# FRANKENSTEIN

## BY MARY SHELLEY

adapted by Larry Weinberg

text illustrations by Ken Barr

HAMPTON-BROWN

THE EXCHANGE

**Why do people
judge others
by the way they look?**

Hampton-Brown
P.O. Box 223220
Carmel, California 93922
800-333-3510
www.hampton-brown.com

Printed in the United States of America

ISBN-13: 978-0-7362-2793-3
ISBN-10: 0-7362-2793-8

12 13 14 10 9 8 7 6 5 4 3 2

TO HEATHER AND MICHAEL
AND LARA AND JANE

# FRANKENSTEIN

**M**y name is Victor Frankenstein. I am the
one who made the Monster. I am **to blame** for
everything. For all those he has killed. For those
who **have gone to bed in fear**. For his being alive
still to this very day.

Yes, I am to blame for what has **become of** the
Monster, too. For all his sadness. And for his hatred
of me.

I am sick now and about to die. So I will tell
you the story. Perhaps YOU will catch the Monster
for me!

---

**to blame** responsible
**have gone to bed in fear** are scared when they sleep
**become of** happened to

*Victor Frankenstein discovers how to create life.*
*He soon realizes what a terrible creature he created.*

# Chapter 1

**I**t all began when I was a young man in school. I wanted to know everything about everything. But most of all, I wanted to know about LIFE. What made things live? What made them able to grow and breathe and move? I wanted to know it. And I tried very hard to find out.

It took me almost six years. But then I learned. At last I knew **the secret of life**! I told no one about it. Not my father, or my brothers. Not even my sweet Elizabeth—the girl I was going to marry.

There was something I had to do first. I wanted to surprise the whole world. I wanted to make a living creature. A creature who could think and laugh and live! I wanted to do what God himself had done when he created people!

.......................................................................................

**the secret of life**  how to make something live

I knew how to put life into a **lifeless** thing. But I did not know how to make a body. How could I put together a body? I went to graveyards. There, I found the bones of dead men. And I took them home to my workroom. From others who had died, I took ears and feet and hands.

I did not like this part of it. At times it made me sick. And I had to **keep** away from people. I didn't want them finding out. Not even my own family, who lived far away from me in the mountains.

I had to make other parts of the creature myself. He was going to be big. Eight feet tall! And stronger than any man or woman on earth.

**At last the time came.** I was ready. It was a cold and gloomy night in November. The room was dark when I went in. The creature lay on the table. It was a thing of death. But soon it would have life! Soon the world would say what a great man I was! So I thought. Ha! What a FOOL I was! But I did not know it then.

....................................................................................

**lifeless** dead; not living

**keep** stay

**At last the time came.** It was now time for me to make the creature.

I lit a candle. Then I set to work.

Many hours passed. The candle **burned low**.
It was midnight. The time, they say, when strange
things happen. And so they did. From the world of
**darkness**, I now **brought forth** life! How I did it I
shall not tell. I shall NEVER tell! It is enough to say
that the creature moved. Its eyelids opened. And
the Thing stared at me.

I do not know what happened to me just then.
And I do not know why. **It was I who** had put those
eyes into its head. It was I who had thought my
creature would be beautiful. But now, when I saw
those eyes! Eyes wet and yellow like drops of ooze!
When I saw that face! A face like the squirming
worms of the grave. And when the Thing sat up! I
could not **stand** to look at it!

And now it was rising and moving toward me!
I felt the hair lift up on the back of my neck. I
jumped away. I turned. I ran! I rushed into my

........................................................................................

**burned low** was melting
**darkness** the dead
**brought forth** created, made
**It was I who** I
**stand** force myself

bedroom and slammed the door. My heart **banged in my chest**. My face was covered with sweat. I was weak. I almost fell to the floor. But I could not let that happen. I had to think. THINK! What could I do? What had I done! How could I **put an end to** this horrible Thing! But I had no answer.

For hours, I walked back and forth across the room. I was tired. I had not slept in days. I could think no longer. My eyes started to shut. I fell onto my bed and I **was lost in sleep**.

---

**banged in my chest** beat loudly
**put an end to** stop
**was lost in sleep** slept

**BEFORE YOU MOVE ON...**

1. **Mood** The feeling of a story is called *mood*. Reread page 9. What makes the mood scary?

2. **Conflict** Reread page 11. What is the problem of this story?

**LOOK AHEAD** Read pages 12–16 to find out why the Monster makes baby noises.

Perhaps I may have slept an hour. I do not know.
But then a sound wakened me. I looked up. There
was something standing by my bed. It was bending
over me. The Monster! It was making noises. Baby
noises! There was a smile on its frightening face. A
baby smile. It was coming closer with its oozy eyes.

I jumped off the other side of the bed. But the door was behind the Monster. I would have to get past the **horrid** thing to escape. The Monster reached out to touch me. As if I were its father! I couldn't stand it. My jacket was hanging on a hook nearby. I pulled it off and threw it in the Monster's face. Those awful yellow eyes were covered!

I ran to the door, into the hall, down the stairs! There was another door. I pushed it open. Then a gate. I pushed that, too. Now I was away from the house. I kept running and running and running. Was it behind me? Was it chasing me? I wouldn't look back. I couldn't look back! I couldn't stand the thought of its touching me! Looking at me!

But I could not keep going on. **My eyes rolled in my head.** Everything began to turn upside down in front of me. And suddenly I smashed into something. It was my very good friend, Clerval.

"My dear Victor," he **exclaimed**, "what is the **matter**?"

...........................................................................................

**horrid** awful, terrible
**My eyes rolled in my head.** I felt sick and dizzy.
**exclaimed** said with surprise
**matter** problem

"Save me! Oh, save me!" I cried.

"Save you from what?" he asked.

"Nothing!" I said, for how could I tell him about the Monster? About that THING I had made?

"But you look so ill. What has happened to you? What are you afraid of?"

"Don't ask me. You must not know! Do you hear me, Clerval?"

But just then I thought I saw the Thing! There was really nothing there. But I must have been **out of my head**.

"It's here! It's here!" I shouted, and I grabbed hold of my friend. "Don't let it touch me! Oh, don't let it come near me!"

"Victor! Victor!" shouted my friend. "Don't be afraid! I will take care of you! Look! I am chasing it away!"

---

**out of my head**  very confused; crazy

Clerval **made believe** that he **drew** a sword. He cut the air with it as if he were fighting someone who was really there.

"Victor, do you see? Look! Look! I have killed it! It's dead, Victor. I've killed it!"

For a moment I believed him. That moment was enough. **For then a darkness came over me. A darkness without dreams.** And I fell to the ground.

........................................................................................

**made believe** pretended

**drew** pulled out

**For then a darkness came over me. A darkness without dreams.** I became very scared then. I knew I was not dreaming.

**BEFORE YOU MOVE ON...**

**1. Character** The Monster thought he was a baby and Victor was his father. What does this show about the Monster?

**2. Viewing** Look at the picture on page 15. How does it help you understand Victor's feelings of fear?

**LOOK AHEAD** Read pages 17–20 to find out what the Monster does next.

*Victor Frankenstein is too sick to leave his friend's house. The Monster tries to find food, a home, and friends. The people he meets are afraid.*

# Chapter 2

**M**y friend took me to his home and **I was put to bed**. After that, I was sick for a very long time. It was months before I was able to speak. But still I would not talk about the Monster or even think of him. For when I did, I got sick again.

But you must want to know what happened to my Creature. And so I will tell you. Later, if I am still alive, you shall learn how I found out.

The Monster did not stay on in my house. Oh, no. He left soon after me **in the dead of night**. He was a giant and a **newborn** child at the same time. He knew nothing. Not who he was or where he

...........................................................................

**I was put to bed**  he made me go to sleep
**in the dead of night**  in the middle of the night; late at night
**newborn**  very young

was going. But the moon **overhead** was like a big balloon. He reached for it and could not touch it. He followed its soft light into the woods. And soon he was lost in a **deep** forest.

The wind blew in the trees. An ice-cold rain began to fall. I had thrown my jacket at the Monster. And he still had it. But that was not enough. He **shivered** in the cold and damp. After a while, he saw the light of a fire. He did not know what a fire was. But he could feel its warmth. And the fire was pretty, too. It changed colors and danced in the air.

There was a man sitting beside it. As the Thing came nearer, the man heard a noise behind him. He turned and looked straight into the Thing's oozy yellow eyes. Into a face he could see through to the bones below!

My Creature was smiling. But the man did not see a smile. He saw the jawbones moving. And

---

**overhead** up in the sky
**deep** large
**shivered** shook

the giant teeth of **long-dead bodies** shining in the firelight. He tried to scream. But **the scream wouldn't come**. In terror he got to his feet—and RAN!

The Creature did not know why the man had been so afraid. Perhaps there was something that HE should be afraid of as well. So he ran away, too.

It was getting light now. Day was starting. As he walked on, he **grew** hungrier and hungrier. But he did not know what food was. Then he saw a little animal eating berries from a tree. He took some also. And that made him feel better. A deer showed him how to drink water from a brook.

After a while, he heard the chirping of birds. It made him happy. And he tried to sing the way they did. But his own sounds were loud and rough. He wasn't sure where they came from and they scared him. So he became silent and hurried away.

Soon snow began to fall. The snow **went on**

---

**long-dead bodies** bodies that had been dead for a long time
**the scream wouldn't come** he could not scream
**grew** became
**went on** fell

until it covered all the berries and the nuts. The air grew colder, too. And now there was no warm place to rest. For three days and nights, my Monster walked **on and on**.

........................................................................................

**on and on** without stopping

**BEFORE YOU MOVE ON...**

1. **Character's Motive** The Monster left Victor's house. Why?

2. **Cause and Effect** Reread pages 18–19. What did the Monster do that scared the man in the woods? What scared the Monster?

**LOOK AHEAD** Read pages 22–25 to find out if the Monster decides to meet other people.

At last the Monster came to a tiny village. It was suppertime. He could smell cooking everywhere. He could see the smoke of warm fires coming from the houses. But should he go into one of them? Was there something to be afraid of? He couldn't wait any longer. There was a large house nearby. From it came small voices, laughing. He opened the door.

The children inside stopped playing at once. Their eyes grew wide. **Their mouths fell open.** He was only trying to be friends when he put out his hands to them. But they screamed with fright. Their mother's eyes closed and she fell to the floor.

A boy climbed out of the window and up to the roof. "It's the Devil! It's the Devil!" he shouted **at the top of his voice**.

People came running from everywhere. The church bells clanged. **Shouts filled the air.** And the Monster was frightened by it all. He turned and ran out of the house. But now the whole town was there.

Some people could not stand to look at him. They screamed and ran away. Others just stood

...........................................................................................

**Their mouths fell open.** They opened their mouths wide.
**at the top of his voice** as loudly as possible
**Shouts filled the air.** People were yelling everywhere.

there. They were shaking so hard that they couldn't move!

But then a man cried out, "The boy is right! It IS the Devil!"

"**Drive him away!** Drive him away!" screamed the boy.

The man picked up a big stone and threw it. It missed. But soon **the air was filled with other flying things**. My Monster was hit and hit again. He tried to get away. But the people were all around him now, throwing stones and logs and bricks. Men **jabbed** at him with long pointed things. An old woman threw a pot of boiling water at his face.

Suddenly, he howled with a sound that was wilder than any beast. He tore a tree out of the ground and swung it at them. Everyone jumped out of the way. He threw down the tree and rushed out of the town.

The people chased him at first. Some of them had guns by then. And they were firing at him. But he ran like the wind and got away from them. He

---

**Drive him away!** Chase him away from here!

**the air was filled with other flying things** people threw more things

**jabbed** poked

was far from town. But he was hurt and in pain. He wanted to lie down. But there was no place. And snow was falling again.

Just then, he saw smoke rising over some treetops. He walked past the trees and came to a little farmhouse. How warm it would be in that little house! How he wanted to go inside! But there would be people in it. And he was so afraid of people now.

Then he noticed something else. **Right up against** the house was a tiny hut. Its roof was too low for even a child to stand inside. Perhaps an animal lived there. He **sneaked up** and looked inside. It was empty!

He crawled into it and lay down. There was no wooden floor. Just earth. But it was dry. My Creature had **gone through so much** since the day that I made him. But now he closed his eyes and went to sleep.

..................................................................................

**Right up against** On the side of
**sneaked up** walked quietly toward it
**gone through so much** experienced many troubles

**BEFORE YOU MOVE ON...**

1. **Character's Motive** The Monster was afraid before he entered the house full of people. Why did he decide to enter?

2. **Character** At first the Monster tried to be friendly. But then he howled and swung at people. Why did he change?

**LOOK AHEAD** Can the Monster think? Read pages 26–31 to find out.

*The Monster hides and watches a loving family.*
*He tries to help and meet them.*
*Once again, he is chased away.*

# Chapter 3

**S**ounds more beautiful than the singing of birds awakened him. But where were they coming from? Not from outside. They were coming from the wall! There was a tiny hole in one wall of the hut. The Monster sat up and looked through it. Now he could see right into the other house!

An old man was sitting inside, playing a guitar. The sounds were so **sweet**, they made the Monster cry. After a while, a young woman came into the room. She brought the old man a plate of food.

"Did you take **anything** for yourself, Agatha?" the old man asked.

......................................................................................

**sweet** beautiful
**anything** some food

"Oh yes," said his daughter. "I have a whole plateful." But this was not true. For she had **taken nothing**. The old man didn't know that because he **was blind**.

Soon the door opened. A young man came into the house carrying wood for the fire. The young woman brought him a plate of food. There wasn't much on it.

"Where is your supper?" he asked his sister.

"Oh," she pretended with a laugh, "I just ate with Father."

"I don't believe you," the young man whispered. "There is enough for both of us." And he gave her half his food.

"Let's not be unhappy, children," said the old man. "The house is warm. And you are strong. And we **have each other**."

Soon everyone was laughing and talking. Then

----

**taken nothing** not taken any food
**was blind** could not see
**have each other** are a family

the old man started to play his guitar again. And all three of them sang.

My Monster listened and listened. What did all those sounds mean? How he wished he **could tell**! Yet there was one thing he did know. Though he did not know words for it. He knew that all the people in that house loved one another. And they **belonged** together.

The Monster decided to stay near them. He would make them his own family. But of course, they must not know it. They might hurt him and chase him away as the others had done. No, they must not see him. But he could see THEM!

So, **day after day**, he sat there in his little hut. And hour after hour, he watched his new family through the hole in the wall. In the daytime, he watched the daughter working in the house. And the old man playing the guitar. In the evening he listened to them singing and talking. He saw them hug and kiss each other. How he wanted to **do that**!

.............................................................................................

**could tell**  knew
**belonged**  should live
**day after day**  after many days
**do that**  hug and kiss someone; be loved, too

He was starting to learn things, too. What "father" meant. And "sister" and "brother." That the woman's name was Agatha. And her brother's name was Felix. He learned the words "fire" and "wood" and "food" and "sleep."

Soon he was learning more and more words. And he was learning other things as well. How people helped one another. And what they thought about. And how sad his friends were because they had become so poor. For now the air was getting colder. Their cow no longer gave milk. And the food they had saved from their garden was almost all gone.

At night, when they were **fast asleep**, the Monster would sneak out of his hut. Then he would **go off** to look for berries and nuts. Very few were left. But he saved most of them for Agatha and Felix

---

**fast asleep** sleeping
**go off** leave

and for their father. In the morning, they would find something to eat lying on their doorstep. And they would wonder how the food got there.

**BEFORE YOU MOVE ON...**

1. **Evidence and Conclusions** The Monster could think. Reread pages 29–30. What shows he could think?

2. **Character's Motive** Reread pages 30–31. Why did the Monster leave berries and nuts on the doorstep?

**LOOK AHEAD** Read pages 32–40 to find out why the Monster throws a rock at himself.

Months passed. Little by little, my Monster taught himself to speak. He wanted to talk as well as they did. If only I can sound like them! he thought. Maybe they will like me and let me stay. The Creature still did not know why people were afraid of him.

But then, one **moonlit night**, he **came across** a pond. He stared into it and saw a face. It was **like none he had ever** seen before. Not like any of those he loved. Not like any animal either. It was horrible. It made him afraid. And he hated it! And now it was looking back at him as if it wanted to kill him!

Quickly he picked up a large rock and threw it at the face in the pond. This Creature had a rock, too! Smash! The face was gone. But then it came back. He smashed it again and again. Each time it returned and did the same things he did. Then, all of a sudden, he knew the truth. HE was the face!

He was a monster! But why? Where did he come from? Who was his family? What kind of **being** was

---

**moonlit night**  night with a bright moon

**came across**  found

**like none he had ever**  different from the faces he had

**being**  creature; living thing

he? He did not know. And he had to **find out**!

Then he remembered something about the jacket he wore. The one that had been thrown at him. There was a notebook in one of the pockets. Perhaps what was written in it would tell him the truth about himself.

The Monster had often watched Felix and Agatha reading aloud to their father. But he did not know how to **do it**. He had to learn to read! But how? For many weeks he tried to teach himself. **But it was no use. No use at all!**

But then one day, Felix brought a young boy to the house. He was the son of a nearby farmer. Felix was going to teach the boy to read!

Here was my Creature's chance. Every day, the Monster studied with the boy. Of course, the boy and Felix did not know it. The Monster worked very, very hard. And soon he was able to read. **At last!** He took the notebook from the jacket pocket. He sat down in the moonlight and read the whole thing.

........................................................................................

**find out** learn

**do it** read

**But it was no use. No use at all!** But he tried and tried and could not do it!

**At last!** Finally!

Everything was in it! All the work that had been done to make him. Now, at last, he knew. The book fell from his hands. His face was covered with tears.

"I have no father and no mother!" he cried. "I am not an animal or a human! I am a thing of the graveyards! I was made to be hated! I hate myself!"

For many days and many nights, he lay in his hut. He did not go out, even to find food. He no longer watched the family through the wall. He wanted to die.

But as he lay there, he began to think about the family. They were such kind and loving people. Perhaps they would not look at his face—but **into his heart**. And the old man was blind. He would never have to look at the Monster at all. He decided to speak to the old man first.

If only the old man will like me, thought my Creature. Then perhaps, perhaps, there is **still a chance**. Still a chance for me to live and be happy like everyone else!

...................................................................................

**into his heart** see his love for them instead
**still a chance** a possibility

One day, when the father was all alone, there was a knocking at the door.

"Come in," said the old man.

"Thank you," answered the Monster, and he went inside. "My name is Frankenstein," he said. "And I am looking for three friends."

"Who are they?" asked the old man.

"The kindest people in all the world. But, **alas**, they do not know me. And I am not like anyone else."

"You say they are kind," replied the old man. "Then **it will not matter to them** that you are different."

"But others have **treated me so badly** that I am afraid."

"Do not be," said the old man. "For I can tell that you are good. And I will help you all I can. Who are these people **whom you seek**?"

The Monster fell on his knees and kissed the old man's hands. "It is you!" he cried. "You and Felix and Agatha whom I love!"

.......................................................................

**alas** unfortunately, sadly
**it will not matter to them** they will not care
**treated me so badly** been so unkind to me
**whom you seek** you are looking for

Just then, the cottage door opened. It was the son and daughter. The Creature turned to them. He wanted to say, "Please don't be afraid of me. I would **die** for you." But it was too late! For Agatha looked at him, then fell to the floor.

Felix grabbed an ax that was hanging on the wall. He swung it with all his **might**. The ax went into the Monster's body. His bones cracked, and he howled in pain. But the Creature got up. He pulled the ax out of his body. He raised it high over the young man's head.

"Don't hurt us! Don't hurt us!" the blind man cried out.

My Monster stopped. He took the ax in both hands and **snapped it in half**. Now it was as broken as his heart. He threw down the pieces and rushed out of the cottage.

"They tried to kill me!" he screamed as he ran. "Those whom I love. The very ones I would have died for! They all hate me! Oh, why was I ever made? Why am I alive?"

......................................................................

**die** do anything
**might** strength
**snapped it in half** broke the ax into two pieces

**A look of anger came over his face.** It was a look that would make the mountains shake in fear. "BECAUSE OF VICTOR FRANKENSTEIN!" he cried.

It was then that the **hatred grew in my Creature's heart**. A hatred that would be the cause of all the horrors I am about to tell.

........................................................................

**A look of anger came over his face.** He became very angry.

**hatred grew in my Creature's heart** Monster started to hate everyone and everything

**BEFORE YOU MOVE ON...**

1. **Plot** The Monster did not know the reflection in the pond was his and he was scared of it. What did he realize when the face kept coming back?

2. **Cause and Effect** Reread pages 38–40. Why did hatred grow in the Monster's heart?

**LOOK AHEAD** Read pages 41–46 to find out if the Monster gets better.

*The Monster tries to find Victor. He meets a boy and wants to be friends. But the boy is scared.*

# Chapter 4

**D**eep in the forest was a cave. There, my Monster lay on a bed of leaves. He could **do little for** himself. And there was no one to help him. But he was very strong. And he began to get better.

At last he was ready to leave. Ready **for** Victor Frankenstein! He had no idea where to find me. But that **did not matter**. For there had been a letter in that jacket of mine. And it told him where my family lived! It was in a town high in the mountains—far away.

When night came, he **set out**. He stayed away from roads. For there are people on roads. And how he hated them all! Following the stars, he

........................................................

**do little for**  not help
**for**  to find
**did not matter**  was not important
**set out**  left to look for me

**made his way** through forests. He crossed wide rivers. He came to the mountains and started to climb. Then, at last, he saw the town.

He was just outside of it, in a **wooded park**. It was time to rest and think about what he would do next. Just then, he heard someone laughing. He quickly hid behind a tree. From his hiding place he saw a young boy. The boy was coming nearer.

Suddenly he thought, The boy is so young that I can teach him. I will take him away with me. And he will learn to be my friend!

As the child came by, the Monster grabbed him. "Don't scream, boy!" said the Thing. "I am not **the way** I look. There is nothing to be afraid of."

But the child was very scared. "Don't eat me! Don't eat me!" he begged.

"I won't eat you. **Hold still!** I only want you to be my friend. But now you must come along with me to the forest."

"You can't take me!" the boy cried. "My father will punish you. He is Mayor Frankenstein!"

.........................................................................

**made his way** walked
**wooded park** place with many trees
**the way** as scary and horrible as
**Hold still!** Do not move!

When the Creature heard this, he lifted the boy into the air. "You are a FRANKENSTEIN? Where is my enemy? Where is Victor Frankenstein?"

My poor brother William kicked and screamed and tried to get away. But the Thing put his hands around William's throat and shook him. True, he only meant to make him **quiet down**. But it was a child's throat! William stopped moving. My dear, sweet little brother was dead!

At first the Monster thought, Oh! What have I done? But then—THEN—he was glad! He laughed and shouted, "This is how I **shall punish my enemy**!" he shook his big fists at the sky and screamed, "I have just begun!"

Around my brother's neck was a little chain. There was a picture of a woman hanging from it. The Monster looked closely at it. The face was lovely. And it made him think of Agatha. He took it from the dead child and left.

A little farther on, the Monster **came upon** a farmer's barn. I can hide here, he thought.

---

**quiet down** be quiet
**shall punish my enemy** will hurt you, Victor
**came upon** saw

Opening the door, he went inside. But the barn was not empty. A young woman lay sleeping on a pile of straw.

Silently, he went closer to look at her. She, too, had a lovely face. A face like Agatha's. Tears came

to his eyes. He bent over her and whispered in her ear, "**Awake**, my dearest love. And **come away** with me forever."

The girl started to turn toward him. And suddenly my Monster became afraid. No! No! I

........................................................................................

**Awake** Wake up
**come away** live

**dare** not wake her, he thought. She will look at me **like all the rest**! She will show me how she hates me! She would never love me—never! Then the Monster grew very angry. And he decided to punish her.

He took the picture and hid it among the sleeping girl's clothes. The police will find this, he told himself. They will think that it was she who killed the little boy. Ha! Ha! They will **put her to death** for it. While I will still be free! Free to laugh and laugh in the face of Victor Frankenstein!

......................................................................................

**dare** should
**like all the rest** the same way everyone looks at me
**put her to death** kill her

**BEFORE YOU MOVE ON...**

1. **Inference** The Monster got better. Then he said that he was "ready for Victor Frankenstein!" What did he mean?

2. **Character** How did the Monster's actions in Chapter 4 show he had changed?

**LOOK AHEAD** Read pages 47–51 to find out what Victor sees that makes him cry.

*Victor finds out that his brother is dead. The Monster killed Victor's brother! But Victor does not tell anyone who the real killer is.*

# Chapter 5

You may wonder what happened to me during all of this. Well, I had been ill for a long time. My friend Clerval had **taken care of me**. But I never told him about the Monster. No, it made me even sicker to talk about it. And Clerval would never have believed me, anyway.

I was getting better when a letter came from my father. "Dear Victor," he wrote. "Your dear little brother William has been killed! The killer took the gold chain William wore around his neck. **From it hung** a picture of your mother. Oh, Victor, William was killed for a gold chain! I need you near me, my son. Please come home **at once**!"

..............................................................................................

**taken care of me**  helped me when I was sick; helped me get better

**From it hung**  On the chain was

**at once**  as soon as you can

I left right away. The trip was long. And I was very sad. I kept thinking about the little brother whom I would never see again.

At last I came to the mountains not far from my father's town. It was night and I was alone on the road. A great storm had started. Thunder **roared over my head**. Lightning flashed in the sky. And, all of a sudden, I saw the Monster!

He was very close. But it all happened so quickly. When the sky **lit up**, I saw him. Then **all went dark**.

Lightning flashed again. Now he was high up. He had already climbed the mountain. **In no time**, he was gone.

I closed my eyes and began to cry. For I now knew who the killer of my brother was. It was the devil that I myself had made!

But there was more horrible news to come. I heard it as soon as I got to my father's house.

........................................................................

**roared over my head**  made a loud sound in the sky

**lit up**  became bright because of the lightning

**all went dark**  it became dark again

**In no time**  Quickly

"Oh, Victor," my father cried out. "It's worse than we thought. The killer lived in our own home. It was Justine, our own maid! The police found her near where William was killed. She was in a barn, pretending to sleep. And she had the chain with your mother's picture!"

"You are wrong, Father," I exclaimed. "It's a mistake! Justine didn't do it!"

"But how do you know?"

I could not answer. He, too, would not have believed me. No one **had ever heard of such a monster before**. And my father knew that I had been ill. He would blame everything I said on my illness.

But my dear Elizabeth was there. And she answered for me. "Because we know what Justine is like," she said. "She loved William very much. And she could never do anything like that!"

-----

**had ever heard of such a monster before** could even imagine a monster like this

On the next day, the trial was held. Justine was brought from the jail. She could not **tell how she came to have** the picture. Only Elizabeth and I believed her story. But there was nothing we could do to save her. Elizabeth begged for Justine's life. But the poor girl was taken to a tree and hanged.

........................................................................

**tell how she came to have** explain why she had

**BEFORE YOU MOVE ON...**

1. **Character's Motive** Victor cried when he saw his Monster. Why?

2. **Cause and Effect** Victor did not tell his family about the Monster. What happened as a result?

**LOOK AHEAD** How can Victor feel sorry for the Monster who killed his brother? Read pages 52–55 to find out.

*Victor and the Monster meet again. The Monster tells Victor about his lonely life. He tells Victor to make a wife for him.*

# Chapter 6

*I* had to be alone. I needed time to think. To find some way to **put an end to all of** this. I took a horse and went into the mountains by myself.

The higher I climbed, the worse the road became. And soon there was no road. I had to leave the horse behind. Up, up I went until there were no more trees. Now there was nothing but ice and snow—and, perhaps, the Monster. Yes, he WAS there! He was waiting for me. . . .

"Devil!" I shouted, and **sprang at him**. But he was too fast for me, I jumped at him again. But again he got away from me. "Killer!" I cried. "Child killer!"

---

**put an end to all of** stop
**sprang at him** ran quickly at him

"You are to blame!" said my Creature. "You who made me! You who gave me this face! I am your own son! But you ran from me! I want you to know what has happened to me!"

"I don't want to hear it!" I said.

"You must! Or I shall kill everyone **dear to you**! **You deserve it.** For I alone cannot be happy! I alone cannot be loved!"

"Very well," I said. "I will listen to your story."

And so the Monster told me all that had happened to him. And do you know, I **was sorry** for him! Yes, sorry for the killer of my own brother and Justine.

When the Creature saw this, he said, "Now you must help me."

"What do you want?"

"A wife! I want a wife! Go back to your graveyards. Make me another like myself!"

"Never!" I cried.

"Never?" said the Monster. "Then I shall kill and kill and kill. And you **shall be the last**."

---

**dear to you** you love

**You deserve it.** It is your fault.

**was sorry** felt bad

**shall be the last** will be the last person I kill

I **thought it over**. I had to do what the Creature wanted. "Will you go away?" I asked. "Will you never hurt anyone again?"

"Why should I hurt anyone if I am happy?"

"You must promise!" I said

"I do promise. I shall go with my wife to a far-off place. No one will ever see us again."

"Then I shall make another **such as you**."

"I shall be watching you," said the Monster. "So **waste no time.**"

---

**thought it over** thought about it
**such as you** monster like you
**waste no time** hurry

**BEFORE YOU MOVE ON...**

1. **Character** Victor felt sorry that the Monster never had love. What will make the Monster feel better? Reread page 54 to find out.

2. **Conclusions** Victor first refused to make the wife. How did the Monster convince him to do it?

**LOOK AHEAD** Does Victor Frankenstein create another monster? Read pages 56–62 to find out.

*Victor begins to make the Monster's wife, but he cannot finish. The Monster is angry, and he promises to return on Victor's wedding night.*

# Chapter 7

**E**lizabeth was waiting for me when I returned home. "I'm so glad you are back!" she cried. "I was so unhappy without you."

"But I can't stay," I told her. "I must go away."

**The smile left her face.** I saw the **hurt** in her eyes. She was thinking that I did not love her any longer. But I did! **More than anything in this world.** Yet how could I tell her why I really had to leave? Could I have said, "I have to go out and **rob** graves. I have to make a second devil!"

I tried to make her feel better. "As soon as I return," I promised, "we will be married." I kissed her and then I left.

......................................................................................

**The smile left her face.** She stopped smiling.

**hurt** sadness

**More than anything in this world.** I loved her very much.

**rob** steal dead bodies from

I had decided to go far, far away. To take a boat and go to another country. To England. Perhaps the Monster would follow me there. I hoped he would. Then **my loved ones** back home would be safe.

No sooner had I started on my trip than I had a surprise. My friend Clerval **turned up beside me**. Elizabeth had asked him to go along with me. But how could I make a creature with him around? And I could never have told Clerval my secret. He would have thought **me mad**.

"I'm well again," I told him. "I don't need anyone to take care of me. You **need not** come along."

Clerval laughed and shook his head. "You can't **get rid of ME!**" he said. "We are going to have some good times whether you like it or not!"

How could I have a good time? I, who had made that Thing of Death? And yet, I felt better when my friend was near. He was the happiest man I ever knew. He could make even the stones smile.

Once we were at sea, I forgot about my Monster. I tried to forget about everything. I looked at the

..................................................................................

**my loved ones**  the people I loved
**turned up beside me**  arrived
**me mad**  I was crazy
**need not**  do not have to
**get rid of ME**  make ME leave

ocean and the sky. I watched the sea gulls fly high into the clouds. How free they were! And I felt free myself!

By the time we got to England, I was happy! Yes, happy! Clerval and I went everywhere. We laughed and sang and made a lot of friends.

But then, one night, I saw the Thing. He was standing on a hill, looking at me. He lifted his long and ugly fingers to his own throat—and squeezed them! My eyes closed. But only fast enough to blink. When they opened again, he was gone! Perhaps I had not seen him. Perhaps I had only dreamed it. But then I heard the laugh. It was a laugh no living thing had ever made before.

I had to get away from my friend. I wrote him a letter. In it was an excuse for my leaving. Then I **slipped away** while he was sleeping. All I took with me were the things I needed to work with. **The time had come.** Now I would make a bride for the Frankenstein Monster.

I went to a place where I could be left alone.

..........................................................................

**slipped away** left quietly
**The time had come.** It was now time for me to start to work.

It was on a small island. I had to sail a little boat to get there. Only a few people lived in the place. I rented a little cabin near an old graveyard. Nobody ever went there. Good!

Day and night I worked at making a wife for my

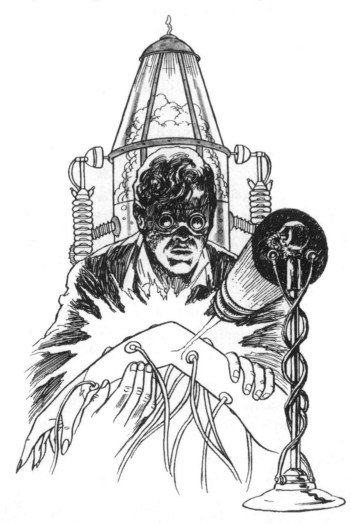

Monster. I wanted to **get it over with**. It made me sick to look at what I was doing. But still I went on with my bones and eyeballs and bits of hair. **It was all going very fast.** And then, one night, there it was! Another horrible Thing on the table! I tried not to think about it. Only a little more to do, and it would be alive.

Soon he would come for her. And they would go away together. No one would ever hear from them again. Everyone would be safe!

But then I thought, What if he was lying to me? And what if they have children? More Monsters! More killers! Together they could destroy the world!

Just then, I heard a scratching sound. It was the Monster at my window! He was looking at **his bride-to-be**. He was waiting. **I couldn't stand it any longer.** Not one more minute! I ran to the table . . . and tore the Thing on it to pieces! Then I threw the pieces of his wife at the window!

The Monster opened his mouth and howled. It

......................................................................................

**get it over with**  be finished

**It was all going very fast.**  I was making the monster very quickly.

**his bride-to-be**  the creature he was going to marry

**I couldn't stand it any longer.**  I could not continue to work on this monster.

was a sound that seemed to come out of the bottom of the earth. I thought he would break the wall and kill me at once. But no, he **dashed down** to the sea. He climbed into a boat and soon was gone.

........................................................................................

**dashed down** ran

I ran out after him and screamed, "I am not afraid of you! Come for me now!"

"Not yet!" **came a voice from across the waves**. "But I will be with you on your wedding night! . . . "

..............................................................................................

**came a voice from across the waves** he said from the boat

### BEFORE YOU MOVE ON...

1. **Setting** Reread pages 58–59. Victor began to create a wife for the Monster. Where did he go to do this? Why?

2. **Foreshadowing** Reread page 62. The Monster ran away when Victor destroyed his wife. What do you think will happen next? Why?

**LOOK AHEAD** Read pages 63–67 to find out why Victor goes to jail.

*Victor's friend is dead. Everyone thinks Victor is the killer, and he goes to jail. Victor is set free when the police learn he could not be the killer.*

# Chapter 8

*I* had to find some way to get rid of the Monster. To kill him before he killed me.

I decided to find my friend Clerval. The time had come to return home with him and marry Elizabeth. So the Monster had promised to kill me on my wedding night? Then let him come, I told myself. This time, I will be ready for him!

That night, I left the island in a sailboat. I had a basket with me. As soon as I could, I threw the basket into the ocean. **Must you really** know what was in it? They were the **filthy** pieces of the wife of the Frankenstein Monster.

How glad I was **to be rid of them**! I had not

---

**Must you really** Do you really want to
**filthy** disgusting, gross
**to be rid of them** that I had thrown them away

slept for days and days. Now I could not keep my eyes open. I fell asleep.

I must have slept for a long time. When I awoke, my boat was touching the English shore. There were people standing around me. I did not like the way they were looking at me.

"What's the matter?" I asked. "Why are you angry with me?"

"You'll find out soon enough!" said a man.

The people grabbed me and took me to a house. Many others were inside. One of them was a judge. He told me that a man had been found dead on the shore. There were finger marks on his neck. He said the killer was a stranger like me. And a boat like mine had been seen going away from the shore.

Suddenly, **my body went cold all over**. And **the hair on my head started to rise**. For a horrible thought had come to me.

"I must see the body!" I shouted.

They took me to it at once. Yes, it was my dearest friend. It was Clerval!

I started to laugh. I couldn't stop laughing. And the truth is, it wasn't me who was laughing. **I sounded in my own ears** like my Monster. No, that wasn't me any longer. For I, Victor Frankenstein, **had lost my mind**.

For two months I lay in a jail. What did it matter? I did not know it. Then, little by little, my mind returned.

......................................................................................

**my body went cold all over**  I felt very cold

**the hair on my head started to rise**  I felt very uncomfortable and scared

**I sounded in my own ears**  I thought I sounded

**had lost my mind**  was not thinking clearly; was crazy

Everybody was kind to me then. For the police had learned that I had not killed my friend. I was still on my island when it had happened.

They let me go. I got on a ship and returned to my country.

**BEFORE YOU MOVE ON...**

1. **Comparisons** How did Victor react to Clerval's death? How had he reacted to the death of his brother?

2. **Conclusions** Why was Victor set free from jail?

**LOOK AHEAD** Read pages 68–73 to find out if Victor tells Elizabeth about the Monster.

*The Monster finds Victor and his new wife on their wedding night. Victor thinks he can stop him. But the Monster wants to kill Elizabeth.*

# Chapter 9

**E**lizabeth and I were married soon after my return home. You may wonder why. Had I forgotten the Monster's warning? "I will be with you on your wedding night!" he had said.

No, I had not forgotten it. But **I'd had enough of** being afraid of him. He will come to kill me, I thought. Fine! Let him come, then. For I will get him first! I had bought two guns and a long sharp knife. I hid them in my clothes and went to my wedding.

It was a beautiful day. And everyone at the wedding was happy. Even I. Later that afternoon, we said goodbye to all and left. Elizabeth had a house **on** a lake. It would take two days to get there.

........................................................................................

**I'd had enough of** I was finished

**on** near

We planned to spend the first night at a hotel along the way.

By the time we got there, **the sun was going down**. I tried to keep smiling. But Elizabeth saw that there was something very wrong.

"Please tell me what it is," she asked. "We are married now, my dearest. You must **not keep secrets from me**."

I had never told her about the Monster. I had never told anyone. Perhaps I should have.

"Tomorrow," I said. "I will tell you everything. I promise." Yes, tomorrow, I thought to myself. When the Monster is dead.

I knew that he would be coming for me soon. And I did not want Elizabeth to have to look at his face. Or perhaps to get hurt in the fight. So I asked her to go to our room and not to come out.

After she left, I began to look around carefully. I went into every hiding place. Behind curtains and stairs and in the **deep**, dark shadows of the hall. There was a clock **standing on** the floor. It was

.................................................................

**the sun was going down** it was getting dark outside
**not keep secrets from me** tell me all of your secrets
**deep** very long
**standing on** on

over eight feet tall. It had a door. I walked toward it. With one hand, I held a gun. With the other, I slowly reached out for the door. Suddenly, I pulled it open. It was empty! The Monster was nowhere to be seen.

And then I heard a scream. Oh, fool, fool, FOOL that I had been! It wasn't me that he had come for. It was Elizabeth! He was with her! In the room!

I ran like a wild animal. I **threw myself** against the door. It broke open. I jumped inside with my gun ready. But it was too late. My Elizabeth . . . my own dear Elizabeth . . . the **heart of my life**! She was . . . she was . . . she was lying on the floor. My Elizabeth was dead.

The killer stood outside the open window. He pointed at the body and laughed. He LAUGHED!

---

**threw myself**  pushed very hard
**heart of my life**  person I loved the most

I fired at him. My shots missed. He was gone. Oh, that devil had taken my brother, my friend, and my wife! **There was nothing left to live for now.** Nothing except to find my enemy and **put an end to him forever**. Now it was I who would be the hunter!

One night, I went to the graveyard where my dear ones were buried. I fell to my knees and cried out to the ghosts. "Help me, oh you spirits of the dead! Lead me to this Thing that I have made! Give me the strength to **wipe him from the face of the earth**!"

From behind me, somewhere, I heard the Monster speak. "Victor Frankenstein! You have killed my wife and I have killed yours. But I am not finished with you yet. We shall play a game, you and I. I shall hide and you **shall seek**. So follow me, then! Follow me **to the ends of the earth**! But you will never find me—until I am ready."

....................................................................................

**There was nothing left to live for now.** I did not want to live.

**put an end to him forever** kill him

**wipe him from the face of the earth** remove him from the world

**shall seek** will look for me

**to the ends of the earth** to places that are far away

I fired my gun into the darkness. But he had already gone. From far off, I heard him laughing.

"Follow me, Victor Frankenstein! Follow me **to your grave**!"

........................................................................

**to your grave** until you die

**BEFORE YOU MOVE ON...**

1. **Conclusions** Reread page 69. Victor did not tell Elizabeth about the Monster. Why did he say, "Perhaps I should have"?

2. **Paraphrase** Reread pages 72–73. In your own words, tell what the Monster said to Victor in the graveyard.

**LOOK AHEAD** Read pages 74–77 to find out why Victor goes to the North Pole.

*Victor follows the Monster. The Monster has punished Victor enough. Victor knows he will soon die and the Monster will be alone.*

# Chapter 10

*A*nd so the great hunt began. I followed him over deserts and mountains and great seas. I followed him north, **ever** north. Toward the lands of snow and ice. There, **the cold wind entered my bones and would not leave**. But I would not rest. I did not sleep. There were times when I did not eat.

Sometimes I came so close to him that I could hear him laughing at me! Yes, still laughing! If only he had stopped laughing, I might have **given up**. But no! He wanted me to follow him!

If I was lost, he would leave a sign to show me the way. Sometimes he even left me food! Yes, he wanted me to stay alive! For the longer I chased

........................................................................................

**ever** always

**the cold wind entered my bones and would not leave** I became very cold

**given up** stopped following him

him, the more he could laugh at me.

At last, I came to the end of land. There was nothing ahead but the North Pole. And ice stretching far out over the ocean. There I learned that he had stolen a dog sled. He had **headed** toward the Pole. I knew why he was leading me there. He was taking me to my place of death.

Well, so be it. We would die together. My Monster and I. I bought a dog sled and set off.

**For days on end**, I crossed the ice. There was nothing but wind and sky. Not an animal. Not a bird. **I was running out of food.** One by one, my dogs were dying of the cold.

And then I saw him! He was far ahead. But he knew I was coming. And he waved at me! I followed! I gave a shout of happiness! At last, I thought! At last I shall finish him!

I drove the dogs on as fast as they could go. But the ice under my sled began to crack. The ocean **reached up** and my dogs fell into it. They were too weak to swim. And they **drowned** in the cold

........................................................................

**headed** started to go
**For days on end** For many days
**I was running out of food.** I had eaten most of my food.
**reached up** came up through the ice
**drowned** died

waters. I was left alone on a floating piece of ice. Alone and turning to ice myself.

But then a ship came by. Sailors saw me and pulled me **on board**. The captain was a kind man. He had me taken to his cabin and put to bed. THIS bed. A bed that I shall never leave while I am alive.

And so my story **nears its end**. For I am dying. **Everything grows dark before my eyes.** I cannot even lift my hand.

........................................................................................

**on board**  into the ship

**nears its end**  is almost finished

**Everything grows dark before my eyes.**  I cannot see well because I am dying.

But what of the Monster whom I never caught? He is out there on the ice—waiting. Soon the moonlight will shine on my **still** face. The Monster will climb toward the ship . . . and come into this cabin.

But when he sees that I am dead, he will not laugh. This time he will not. No, he will fall down on his knees and howl with sadness. For I am his father. I am the one who **gave him life**. And the only one who could ever have loved him.

The Monster will be alone.

**still** dead
**gave him life** created him

**BEFORE YOU MOVE ON...**

1. **Character's Motive** The Monster led Victor to the dangerous land of snow and ice. Why did Victor continue to chase him?

2. **Character's Point of View** Reread page 77. How does Victor feel about the Monster when he is dying at the end of the story?